Goha and His Donkey

An Egyptian Folktale

retold by Amany Hassanein
pictures by Valeri Gorbachev

Richard C. Owen Publishers, Inc.
Katonah, New York

The donkey got tired,
so . . .

Goha walked down the street.
His son rode their donkey.

3

Goha heard someone say,
"Look how Goha spoils his son."

So Goha rode the donkey
and his son walked.

Then Goha heard someone say,
"Goha is unkind.
He makes his son walk."

So Goha and his son
rode the donkey.

Then Goha heard
someone say,
"Goha is unkind to his donkey."

So Goha and his son
walked beside the donkey.

Then Goha heard someone laugh,
"Goha is foolish.
He has a donkey and doesn't ride it!"

And then Goha knew that
he could not please all the people
all the time.

So Goha said . . .
"Whoever gets tired shall ride."

13